W9-CMF-628

READ ALL THESE

NATE THE GREAT DETECTIVE STORIES

AND CONTINUE THE DETECTIVE FUN WITH

OLIVIA SHARP

by Marjorie Weinman Sharmat and Mitchell Sharmat
illustrated by Denise Brunkus

Nate the Great

Talks Turkey

With help from Olivia Sharp

by Marjorie Weinman Sharmat
and Mitchell Sharmat

illustrated by Jody Wheeler
in the style of Marc Simont

Delacorte Press

Published by
Delacorte Press
an imprint of
Random House Children's Books
a division of Random House, Inc.
New York

Text copyright © 2006 by Marjorie
Weinman Sharmat and Mitchell Sharmat
New illustrations of Nate the Great,
Sludge, Claude, Oliver, Rosamond, the
Hexes, Annie, Fang, Harry, Esmeralda,
Finley, and Pip by Jody Wheeler based upon
the original drawings by Marc Simont.
All other images copyright © 2006 by Jody Wheeler.

Special Guest Appearances by Olivia Sharp and Willie the Chauffeur
from the Olivia Sharp, Agent for Secrets series
by Marjorie Weinman Sharmat and Mitchell Sharmat

The trademark Delacorte Press is registered in the U.S. Patent and Trademark Office and
in other countries.

Visit us on the Web! www.randomhouse.com/kids
Educators and librarians, for a variety of teaching tools, visit us at
www.randomhouse.com/teachers

Library of Congress Cataloging-in-Publication Data
Sharmat, Marjorie Weinman.
  Nate the Great talks turkey / Marjorie Weinman Sharmat and Mitchell Sharmat ;
illustrated by Jody Wheeler.
    p. cm.
  Summary: Nate the Great and his cousin Olivia are on the case of a runaway turkey.
  ISBN-13: 978-0-385-73336-6 (trade)—ISBN-13: 978-0-385-90353-0 (glb)
  ISBN-10: 0-385-73336-4 (trade)—ISBN-10: 0-385-90353-7 (glb)
  [1. Turkeys—Fiction. 2. Mystery and detective stories.] I. Sharmat, Mitchell. II.
Wheeler, Jody, ill. III. Title.
  PZ7.S5299Nay 2006
  [Fic]—dc22
                2006002077

The text of this book is set in 17-point Goudy Old Style.
Book design by Trish Parcell Watts
Printed in the United States of America
May 2007
10 9 8 7 6 5 4 3

Chapter One

My name is Nate the Great.
I am a detective.
My dog, Sludge, is a detective too.
This morning we did not have
any cases to solve.
We were eating breakfast
and listening to the radio.
I was eating pancakes.
Sludge was eating a bone.

It was a nice, quiet, tasty morning.
"There is not much news
on the radio," I said to Sludge.
Sludge kept crunching his bone.
Suddenly I heard something.
"A giant turkey is sitting on a car in a
supermarket parking lot.
The people inside the car cannot get out.
There is panic in the parking lot."
"Do you believe that?" I asked Sludge.
Sludge looked puzzled.
I heard a knock at the door.
I got up and opened it.
Claude was there.
Claude is always losing things.
He is one of my best clients.
"I found something," he said.
"You *found* something?" I asked.
"Yes."
"Tell me about it," I said.

"Well," Claude said, "I was walking
in Deering Woods about three hours ago
and I found this really big turkey.

Big feathers, big feet, big everything.
He started to follow me,
but then I lost him.
So, can you find him?"
"Actually, I believe I can," I said.
"But why would you want him?"
"Well, that turkey made me think
about Thanksgiving Day.
Thanksgiving Day is terrific."

"Perhaps the turkey has a different opinion about that day," I said.

"Besides, this is summer.

Thanksgiving Day is months away."

"I still want that turkey," Claude said.

"I *found* him and I am very proud of that."

"I, Nate the Great, understand.

Good work."

"Thank you," Claude said.

"Now how can you help me?"

"I, Nate the Great, say that your really big turkey is in a supermarket parking lot."

"You are a great detective," Claude said.

Sludge looked at me.

He knew I was not a great detective in this case.

"Sludge and I heard about the turkey on the radio," I said.

"The radio?" Claude said.

"I found a *famous* turkey?

I am even better at finding
than I thought."
"My radio is still on," I said. "Let's listen."
Claude, Sludge, and I stood by the radio.
Soon we heard, *"The giant turkey has fled
the supermarket parking lot.
Be on the lookout!
Do not approach him.
He is feathered and dangerous."*
Claude groaned. "He's gone again."
"Yes," I said. "And he could be angry
or scared. You must be careful."

"Oh, no," Claude said. "He's a really nice turkey. A nice, nice turkey."

"Hmmm," I said. "What makes him nice three times over?"

"Well, I was eating popcorn in the woods," Claude said.

"And I dropped some
along the way and he ate it.
Then he started to follow me.
I gave him more popcorn,
until I didn't have any left.
He still followed me.
That's when I knew he liked me.

But later on, when I turned around,
he was gone.
Will you take the case?"
"I can't," I said. "Nate the Great does not
take cases that everybody else is on.
The whole town must be looking
for this turkey."
"Oh," Claude said. He seemed sad.
Sludge put his head on my lap.
He looked sad too.
I patted Sludge. "You want this case,
don't you?" I said.
Sludge wagged his tail.

Chapter Two

"Sludge is a sniffer," Claude said.
"I could use a sniffer on this case.
A detective sniffer."
Claude pulled a white feather
from his pocket.
He put it near Sludge's nose.
"I picked this off the ground
in the woods," he said.
"It must have come from the turkey."

Sludge sniffed the feather.

I, Nate the Great, was thinking.

This was Sludge's chance to work alone.

And he wanted this case.

"You can do it," I said to Sludge.

"You are a dog.

You are a detective.

You are great at being both."

Sludge led Claude out the door.

Chapter Three

The telephone rang.
This quiet day
was no longer quiet.
I picked up the receiver.
"I hope you are on this case," a voice said.
It was my cousin Olivia Sharp.
Olivia lives in San Francisco.
She is also a detective.
She has a chauffeur named Willie.
I know him well.
She has an owl named Hoot.
I know her well too. Unfortunately.
Olivia loves birds.
But she couldn't be calling about the turkey.

"I am calling about the turkey," Olivia said.

"What?" I said. "You heard about him
in San Francisco?"

"Actually, the news is national.
I am on my way to help."

"But . . . ," I said.

Olivia hung up.

Olivia does not like to hear *buts*.

She was determined to come.

What was she up to?

Olivia usually has more cases
than she can handle.

Why would she take time out for a turkey?

Chapter Four

Let me introduce myself.
My name is Olivia Sharp.
My friends call me Olivia.
My enemies call me Liver.
I have an owl named Hoot.
We live in a penthouse
at the top of Pacific Heights
in San Francisco
with my chauffeur, Willie,
my housekeeper, Mrs. Fridgeflake,
and my folks.

But my folks aren't home much.
Right now they're on vacation
on Nantucket Island.
And me?
I was sitting in my office,
looking out the window,
watching the fog as it hung
over Alcatraz and the bay.
I was waiting for business.
I'm a special kind of detective.

An agent for secrets.
But business was slow.
I'd hit a dry spell.
I was bored.
Maybe it was time for *me*
to take a vacation.
I called Willie.
"Pack your bags. Order the plane!
We're going to join my folks
in Nantucket."

I hung up.
My folks own a private airplane.
Willie is a pilot as well as a chauffeur.
I walked out of my room
and closed the door behind me.
"Good-bye, slow business;
hello, fast vacation," I said.
Mrs. Fridgeflake helped me pack my bags.
Willie brought the limo around.
"Everything is set to go, Miss Olivia,"
he said.
I tossed my boa around my neck and
got into the limo.
We were off.

Chapter Five

We were in the air.
I watched the clouds go by
and ate a watercress sandwich
that Mrs. Fridgeflake had packed.
There wasn't much to do.
I got tired of looking at clouds.
I turned on the TV.
I kept changing channels.
Dull, dumb, ho-hum.

I switched to the news.
There was a picture of a giant turkey
sitting on top of a car
in a supermarket parking lot.
I turned up the sound on the television.
I heard the word *panic*.
I heard *"Catch him! Catch him!"*
I sighed. Poor bird.
This turkey was having a worse day
than I was.

Suddenly he disappeared from the screen.

If I were that turkey,

I wouldn't stick around either.

What city was this happening in?

I had missed that part of the story.

I looked closer at the screen.

I kept looking.

I knew that parking lot!

I knew that supermarket!

And suddenly I was back in business.

I made a quick phone call.

Then I went up to Willie.

"Change of plans," I said.

"Back to San Francisco, Boss?" he asked.

"Not exactly, Willie.

I was just talking to Nate the Great.

I think we should drop in on him.

He needs help with a turkey."

Chapter Six

I, Nate the Great,
heard a knock at my door.
What now?
Sludge and Claude were off on a case.
Olivia was on her way from San Francisco.
Meanwhile, I was having
a good, quiet time again.
I was reading a book.
There was no more knocking.
There was pounding.
Somebody out there was in a hurry.
I opened the door.
Olivia was standing there.

"You're *here?*"
I said.
"Where did you
call me from?"
Olivia stepped inside.
"I was up in the air," she said.
"Willie and I flew into town.
We hired a limo,
and he's out there cruising for clues.
Now let's talk turkey."
"Sludge is looking for the turkey," I said.
"And Sludge will find the turkey.
I believe in him."
Olivia crossed her arms.
"Now, listen carefully," she said.
"Birds are my specialty.
That poor turkey is in trouble.

27

I need a list of your friends
for my turkey search team."
"Wait a minute," I said.
"My friends are not detectives."
"Names, please," she said.
I shrugged. "Well, there's
Oliver next door.
He always follows people.

And he can show you
where to find
Rosamond and Annie.

There's also Claude,
but he's already
looking for the turkey
with Sludge."

"Where are they looking?"

"In Deering Woods.

That is where Claude first saw the turkey."

"He *saw* the turkey? Fantastic!"

Olivia tossed her boa into the air.

She wears that boa

just about everywhere.

"Not so fantastic," I said. "Claude also

lost the turkey."

"And *I* will find it again," she said.

And she was out the door.

Chapter Seven

The minute I left Nate's house,
someone started to walk behind me.
I knew who it was.
Oliver the Follower.
I turned around.
"Nobody follows Olivia Sharp," I said.
"I follow everybody," Oliver said.
"How about a turkey?" I asked.
"I need a search team to help me
look for a turkey."
"You mean that famous turkey?
I can't join the team. I haven't seen him,
so I can't follow him."

"I would like to follow you," I said.
"To Rosamond's house."
"Follow me? People just don't do that around here."
I flung my boa around Oliver.
"Let me be the first."
"Actually, you're the second or third," Oliver said.
He started walking.
I started following.
Oliver led me to Rosamond's house.

Chapter Eight

Oliver and I were standing in front
of Rosamond's house.
I was trying to figure out
exactly what I was looking at.
I saw a sign in the front yard.
RENT-A-PET
A NICKEL AN HOUR
I saw a table.
A girl was sitting behind it.
She looked very strange.

Four cats were crawling over the table.
They looked strange too.
"That's Rosamond," Oliver said.
"And her four cats."
Oliver walked away.
I walked up to the table.
"Hello," I said. "I'm Olivia Sharp
and I'm forming a search team
to look in Deering Woods
for the famous turkey.
I would like you to join."

Rosamond pointed to her cats.

"I am running a business here," she said.

"I can't leave.

In fact, I have even more pets to rent.

They are not here right now.

Meanwhile, would you like to rent
one of my cats?

Plain Hex, Little Hex, Big Hex,
or Super Hex?

Choose. They are all fine choices."

"I'm a bird person," I said.

"Birds?" Rosamond said.

"I'll be renting birds."

I started to fidget with my boa.

I had traveled hundreds of miles for *this*?

I had to rethink my situation.
Oliver didn't want to join the team.
Rosamond didn't want to join the team.
And right now I had no team to join.
"Can you tell me where Annie lives?"
I asked.
"You won't have to go there,"
Rosamond said.
"I see her and her dog, Fang,
down the street.
Annie and Fang go everywhere together."
I flicked my boa at Rosamond and left.

Chapter Nine

I walked up to Annie and Fang.
"Hello," Annie said. "You must be
Nate the Great's cousin from
San Francisco."
"How did you know?"
"Well, he told me about the boa.
I haven't seen any others around here."
"Good observation. Olivia Sharp here."
"I'm Annie, and this is my dog, Fang."
I looked at Fang. He was big.
He had lots of soft fur
and his eyes were warm and friendly.

"What a pretty dog!" I said.

Suddenly Annie got excited.

"Oh, you really think so?
I always knew it, but nobody else
ever said it until now."

Annie knelt down close to Fang.

"Thank Olivia and give her a big smile."

Fang opened his mouth.

I immediately knew that he
was perfectly named.

I had never seen fangs like his before.

Awesome! Outstanding! Breathtaking!

And totally unfit for a turkey hunt.

I said, "I must be going. I see my limo
coming to pick me up."

I patted Fang on his head.

A good three inches from his fangs.

Then I left and got into the limo.

"No turkey team," I said to Willie.

"Drive on!"

Chapter Ten

I, Nate the Great, was eating more
pancakes.

I missed having Sludge sitting by me
eating a bone.

I had to think.

Sludge was off trying to help Claude
find a turkey.

Olivia was off trying to find the turkey too.

I, Nate the Great, was just sitting here.

Waiting. And waiting.
I do not like to wait.
But this wasn't my case.
Still, I was curious.
What was going on with that turkey?
I finished eating
and turned on the radio.
There was no turkey news.
I turned on the television.
A reporter was speaking.
"Where is this wild, weird turkey?
Nobody knows. Could this be the turkey who
once ate the entire ant population and one
half of the corn supply of Portland, Maine?"
Hmmm. I, Nate the Great,
had never heard of a turkey
who fit that description.

But I kept watching the screen.
A picture of the turkey flashed on.
He was moving fast.
And now, so was I.
That turkey had given me a clue.
Now I knew I couldn't sit and wait.
I had to find Olivia.

Chapter Eleven

I wrote a note to my mother.

Dear Mother,
I am not on a case.
Sludge is. Olivia
Sharp is. They are
on a Turkey Hunt
I do not want to
go on. But now
I have to go on
my own hunt. I,
Nate the great, can't
wait! I will be
back. Love,
Nate the great

I rushed out.

I saw Oliver in front of his house.

"Have you seen my cousin Olivia?"
I asked.

Oliver nodded.

"Yes," he said. "She asked me to be
on her turkey team. But I can't.
I showed her where Rosamond lives.
Then I went home."

"I must go to Rosamond's house," I said.

"I must follow you," Oliver said.

Chapter Twelve

I saw Rosamond sitting behind
a table in her front yard.
There was a sign on the table.
RENT-A-PET
A NICKEL AN HOUR
Rosamond's cats were crawling
all over the table.
I could see that Rosamond
was in business again.

I wanted to walk away.
But I walked up to her.
"You have a new business, I see."
"Yes," Rosamond said. "Pets need
a change now and then.
Sort of a vacation.
Just like the rest of us.
So I rent them out by the hour."
"There is not much to choose from," I said.
"Only your cats."
Rosamond held up a piece of paper.
"Well, I'm also taking orders.
Here is a list of all
the creatures I can supply."

I, Nate the Great, did not want
to read Rosamond's list.
"What I want to know," I said,
"is where I can find Olivia Sharp."
"Oh, her," Rosamond said. "She left
without renting even one of my Hexes.
Then I saw her talking to Annie and Fang,
and then she went off in a limo."
This was not good news.
Olivia was cruising the streets
looking for the turkey.
I would never be able
to catch up
with her.

"Is there anything else you can tell me?"
I asked Rosamond.
"Well, she wanted me to be
on some kind of turkey team.
But I am busy here. Anyway, I already
have a turkey on my list."
Rosamond pushed the piece of paper
into my hand.
"It's in alphabetical order."
I, Nate the Great, know that
sometimes detectives have to do
strange things.
This was one of those times.
I had to look down at Rosamond's list.
It was alphabetical, all right.
I found *turkey* between *scorpion*
and *vulture*.
I, Nate the Great,
was getting nowhere.

"Are you telling me that you can get these creatures?"

Rosamond sighed. "Well, the vulture might be a problem."

"Where would you get a turkey? There are no turkey farms around here."

Rosamond smiled. Her smiles are strange. Everything about her is strange.

"Well, I asked Annie's brother, Harry, who asked Esmeralda, who asked Finley, who asked Pip, who asked a friend who owns a turkey that was given to her by her uncle."

"What does the turkey look like?"

"He's big and plump
and white and cheery."
Rosamond grinned.
"I plan to charge ten cents
an hour for him."
"So you've seen
this turkey?" I asked.
"Not exactly,"
Rosamond said.
"But Pip's friend told Pip,
who told Finley, who told Esmeralda,
who told Harry, who told me that
that's what the turkey looks like."
"So where is this turkey?" I asked.
Rosamond shrugged. "He's very late.
He should have been here by now.
The anteater is late too."
"The anteater?"
"Top of the list," Rosamond said.

"Do you know who owns this turkey?"
I asked.
"No. But I can ask Harry, who can ask—"
"Never mind," I said. "Do you know
where this turkey lives?"
"Yes. Near Deering Woods,
in a house on Kenwood Street.
I don't know which house."
"Thank you for the information," I said.
I walked away.
"Wait!" Rosamond called. "Is Sludge
available for rent?"
I walked faster.

Chapter Thirteen

I, Nate the Great, was now on a case,
whether I wanted to be or not.
I knew things.
But not enough.
I knew that Kenwood Street
was a long, long street.
I knew that I did not want to go
to every house on it.
I walked to Lowell's Feed and
Pet Supply Store.

I went up to a man behind a counter.
"Do you sell turkey food
to a house on Kenwood Street?"
"Turkey food?" the man said.
"Everybody's talking turkey today."
"Right. But I'm asking about a
specific house."
"Oh, that's private information,"
the man said. "I can't tell you that."
I, Nate the Great, needed that
information.

How could I get it?
I smiled. "Your turkey food must be very
good," I said. "Because that Kenwood
Street turkey is big and plump
and white and cheery."
The man smiled. "Why, yes, you noticed!
We have wonderful food here.
Well, I guess it's easy
to forget a street address
and hard to forget
what good food we sell.

My friend, the address
is Fifty-eight Kenwood Street."
"Thank you," I said.
"Thank *you*!" the man said.
I walked out of the store.
Sometimes a detective can get
information just by giving information.
I hurried over to 58 Kenwood Street.
Should I go up and knock on the door?
No.
I walked around to the side of the house.
Would I get a surprise?
No.
I saw just what I thought I would see.
A large white turkey inside a wire fence.
And outside, looking very happy,
was Sludge.

Chapter Fourteen

I was *so* glad to be back in the limo.
Cool and comfortable.
Nobody following me,
no cats for rent,
and no fangs.
All in all, really, really cool.
But I had no search team.
And Willie had bad news.
Well, actually, Willie had no news.

Whoever said that no news is good news
didn't know what he was talking about.
Willie looked glum.
"I drove around, Miss Olivia," he said,
"but I didn't see anything
that looked like a turkey."
I leaned back in the soft leather seat.
"Not to worry, Willie," I said.
"We don't give up easily."
"So, where to, Boss?"
"Into the woods on foot, Willie.
You and I will go up and down
every path."
"Sounds like a plan," Willie said.
Willie drove down a few streets
and around a corner and parked.
We went into Deering Woods.
There were paths.
And paths.
And paths.

So many choices!
Ugh!
"It would have been terrific
if my team plan had worked out," I said.
Willie knocked some dirt off his shoes.
"Extremely terrific, Boss."

Chapter Fifteen

I, Nate the Great, took a bone
out of my pocket.
"Good work, Sludge," I said.
"You found the turkey."
Sludge wagged his tail
and started to eat the bone.
I examined the wire fence.
It had a big patch in it.
The turkey must have escaped through
what had been a hole in the fence.

Then he came back.
I turned to Sludge.
"Where is Claude?" I asked.
Sludge got up and walked to a path.
I followed.
Sludge put his nose in the dirt.
"I see," I said. "Turkey tracks
going away and coming back
and dog tracks coming.

You followed the turkey tracks here,
and you left dog tracks beside them.
Triple tracks for Claude to follow.
Very good work.
But why isn't he with you?"
I, Nate the Great, didn't have to
ask that question.
I already knew the answer.
Claude had lost Sludge.

And Sludge knew that if he went back
to look for Claude,
he would mess up the tracks.
If he took another path,
he would leave dog tracks
going away from this place.
Not a good idea.
So he was waiting here.
Sludge started to bark. And bark.
Sludge was still on the case.
"Of course!" I said. "You are trying
to *tell* Claude where you are."
Sludge wagged his tail again.
Hmmm.
I, Nate the Great, had an idea.
"Sludge, you bark and
then I'll call Claude's name.
That will make two loud sounds."
"Ready, set, go!"
Sludge barked and I called, "Claude!"

"Now we have to go hide
behind some trees," I said.
Sludge and I ran into the woods.
"Watch for Claude," I said.
We peered out from behind the trees.
Nothing was happening.
We waited.
Then Sludge's ears perked up.
We peered out again.
Nothing.
Suddenly we saw Claude.

Claude saw the turkey.
Claude jumped into the air.
"I found you, I found you!" he yelled.
I, Nate the Great, smiled.
Claude was no longer a loser.
At least for today.
Sludge's ears perked up again.
We heard voices.
Olivia, with her boa dragging in the dirt,
and Willie, huffing and puffing,
staggered out of the woods.

Chapter Sixteen

Olivia walked up to Claude.

Claude was yelling, "I found the turkey!"

Olivia looked at the turkey.

"You found *that* turkey?" she asked.

"Yes, I did," Claude said.

"You even saw me do it."

"Yes, I did," Olivia said.

"And so did Willie here."

Willie nodded.

Olivia wiped her face with her boa.

"You must be Claude," she said.

"And that turkey in the yard

looks like a fine turkey.

Nice-looking, and he probably
has very good manners,
and is, all in all,
a very wonderful turkey."
Then Olivia stamped her foot
and raised her voice.
"But he's not the turkey
I've been looking for!"
Sludge and I stepped out of the woods.
"Congratulations, Claude," I said.
I turned to Olivia.
"I've been trying to find you.

I have something important to tell you."
"Which is?"
"I found out that there were
two missing turkeys.
And Claude's is not the one
you were looking for.
I didn't find out until
I turned on the television
and saw the famous turkey.
Its feathers are dark green
and dark red and other colors.

Claude had shown Sludge
a feather from the turkey he found.
It was white."
Olivia picked up her boa.
"Just a little setback," she said.
"But that won't stop Olivia Sharp.
See you later."
Olivia turned to go.
Willie followed her.
Then he turned around.
"Good to see you and Sludge again,
Mr. Great," he said.
Olivia tugged at his sleeve,
and they were gone.
"Time for us to go," I said to Claude.
He kept looking at the turkey.
"This turkey belongs to somebody else,"
I said. "However, you might be able
to rent him. Check with Rosamond."

Chapter Seventeen

I dusted off my boa
before I got back into the limo.
Then I relaxed in the seat
and sipped orange juice
and ate cheese and crackers.
I took off my shoes and wiggled my toes.
It felt good.
I was ready to resume my hunt.
I needed to find that turkey.
I really, really like birds.
Not only do I own an owl,
but I have also owned a turkey
and some other feathered creatures.
I definitely know turkeys well.
That's why I know I'll find this one.
After all, I'm a detective
and I deal with a lot of secrets.

But now I had to think
about a turkey's secrets.
Get into his mind.
How much was really going on in there?
I'd read that there are vast empty spaces
in a turkey's brain.
I'd also heard that
there are small empty spaces in there.
Nothing I couldn't handle.
I settled back in my seat.
"Onward, Willie!"

Chapter 18

Sludge and I walked home.
I turned on the television
to check on the famous turkey.
I hoped Olivia would be the one
to find him.
But he was still missing.
A reporter was making an announcement.
"Anyone who has seen or knows the
whereabouts of this turkey,
please call 555-0530."

I turned off the television.
Sludge and I went into the kitchen.
I made pancakes and gave Sludge
another bone.
I liked having him there while I ate.
I thought about the turkeys.
Two turkeys missing
at the same time
in the same town.
Two *very big* turkeys
missing at the same time
in the same town.
What seemed logical?
Only one turkey was missing.
That's what I had thought.
That's what Olivia had thought.
But sometimes when everything
seems to fit,
you still have to look for what doesn't fit.
In this case, it was feathers.

Sludge and I finished eating.
We left the kitchen.
I turned the television set back on.
And there was Olivia on the screen,
staring me in the face!

Chapter Nineteen

Olivia was sitting on top of a limo
and the famous turkey was beside her.
The turkey looked happy,
stuffed and groggy.
A reporter came on the screen.
A man was standing next to her.
I knew that man.

The reporter said, "I have here Mr. Lowell from Lowell's Feed and Pet Supply Store. Mr. Lowell, is it true that Olivia Sharp, presently sitting on the limo behind us, walked into your store and purchased $1,864.74 worth of turkey food?"

Mr. Lowell gave a sly grin. Then he said,
*"We never, ever give out private information
to anyone about our customers."*
Mr. Lowell looked proud.
I, Nate the Great, rolled my eyes.
Then the reporter turned to Olivia.
*"And now here we have Olivia Sharp of
San Francisco, who, with the help of her
chauffeur, Willie, caught the turkey that
has been driving this town crazy.
Olivia, is it true that you rode around in
this limo while you sprinkled three hundred
pounds of turkey food in special places
that you knew would attract a turkey?
And then, after only ten minutes,
you found the turkey greedily
gobbling away?"*

Olivia flipped her boa.
It looked clean on television.
Then she said, "*That is a professional
secret. I used my great knowledge of birds
and what they like. But I can say this: I took
this turkey on as my client. I did what I knew
was best for him. He was hungry and he was
hiding out. That is not a good lifestyle for a
turkey. Now he has a full stomach and a
great future.*"

Two hours later
Olivia knocked on my door.
I opened it.
"Turkey-hunting season is over," she said.
"Case closed."
I looked over Olivia's shoulder.
"I, Nate the Great, say there are
some cases that *never* close."